Balboa Press books may be ordered through booksellers or by contacting:

Balboa Press
A Division of Hay House
1663 Liberty Drive
Bloomington, IN 47403
www.balboapress.com.au
1 (877) 407-4847

ISBN: 978-1-5043-1667-5 (sc)
ISBN: 978-1-5043-1711-5 (e)

Print information available on the last page.

Balboa Press rev. date: 03/15/2019

BALBOA.
PRESS
A DIVISION OF HAY HOUSE

ZOEY
and
AMANDA

ASHA HUSSEIN

- Once upon a time there was a girl named Amanda and she has a older sister named Zoey they are from Hawaii they lived in Hawaii for ten years and they also travelled all around the world but now they live in Perth Western Australia and they are enjoying the new experience and the new change with their parents and their four siblings but Amanda didn't like the change she hated every part of the experience but forced her self to love and enjoy the change Amanda's parents said to her to try to enjoy it and fake it until you make it but Amanda ends up liking Australia and enjoying her life and making new friends for her new life Amanda and Zoey started university in 2012 Amanda studied

- writing and publishing and Zoey studied physiology but their parents told them to study nursing but the girls said no because they decided to follow their dreams and goal because its their passion and Amanda also studied arts in fashion and also opened her own family fashion shop all around Australia and America but one day the girls went up to their parents and said that there moving out so that they can live on their own and chase their own dreams but the next day the girls

- went to there friends house to pick up there younger brother and after they picked him up they went back home so the girls can study for their exams and tests so that they can pass and achieve their dreams and goals in 2013 Zoey went to the aquarium to learn about the different kind of animals and the foods that the animals eat she build a friendly relationships with the animals and her co workers but she developed a great peer group to champion her on for her career. But one day they went inside a portal to world were she does acting and dancing. She also does singing witch she love do.

- One day the girls started going on tour and they booked a tour bus for their first ever concert ever but it didn't go very well at all but they kept trying until they got it right one day Amanda and her siblings went down to the bell tower and the Elizabeth quay to go on the boats and to experience the new countries all around the world they said that the world is there's one day the girls convised everyone that there were related an because and no believed them that there were related but the people started believing the girls. But one day Amanda's children came to see there auntie Zoey and their uncle mike but they never met their grandparents witch is very sad and made them very angry. On the year 17_12_1995 it was the year that there were born they celebrated there birthday on different days it turns out

- Amanda and Zoey are not twins Zoey had her birthday with her dad and Amanda had her birthday with her mum there parents broke up for known reason and the girls didn't even know that there were twin sisters

- after a while the girls realized that there were not twin sisters but there were at there parents house waiting for them to get back home so that they can solve there problem because there's a lot off them and find a way to reflect on it and accept it and also to move on from there lives.

- one day the girls and their brother got back from a road trip on their sisters concert but their parents got mad at them because they didn't listen to their parents when their parents left the kids sneaked out off the house to go to the kids show concert in the city with their younger siblings. The kids show started at 6.30pm and it finished at 9.30pm but the older kids got in trouble by their parents and grandparents as well but they were getting grounded for three months after three months the older kids weren't allowed to go out without their parents permission they only leave the house with parents.

- On one sunny summer day the family went downtown to Portland organ the whole family really enjoyed staying in portland organ for the holidays the family love to travel everywhere and meet different people from different cultures all around the world it was very special and magical to see and meet everyone all around the world The whole family loved it so much that they decided to live in portland organ but couldn't live there instead they stayed for six months for the holidays it was for the whole family to enjoy there holiday and to getaway from Australia Perth. The whole family came back from their six's months holiday it was an a amazing holiday with the family. The girls stayed at the hamptons after three weeks.

Amanda and Zoey are really enjoying living in the hamptons at the valley around 22 years off age the girls got married and had kids to look after and lived happily ever after the end.

- Be Bright
- Be the light
- Be kind
- Be loyal
- Be caring
- Be loving
- Be happy
- Be enthusiastic
- Be beautiful
- Be smart
- live
- You can achieve anything and everything
- Children's story by

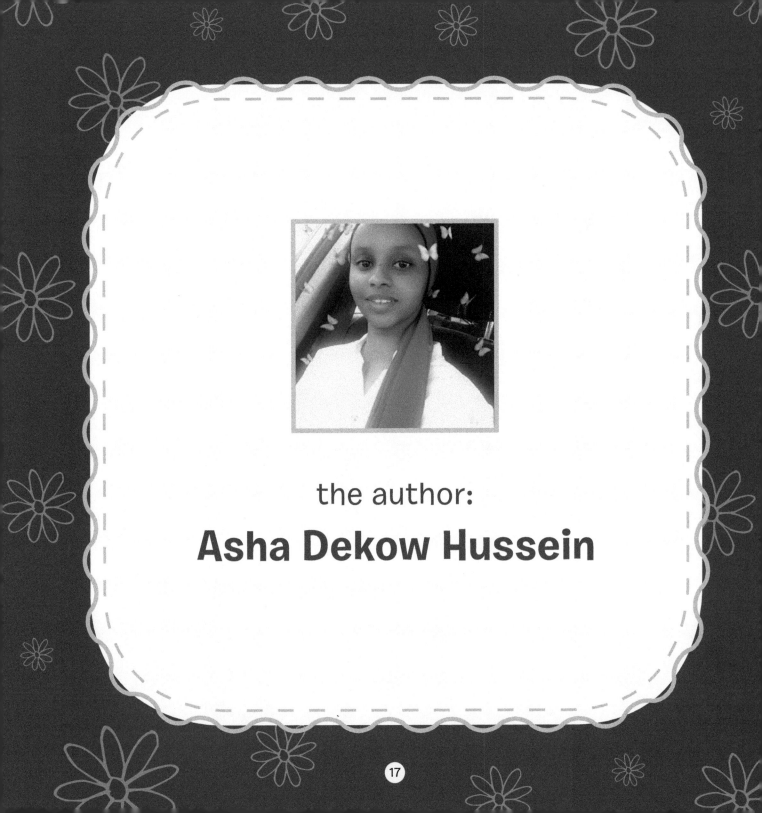

the author:

Asha Dekow Hussein

CPSIA information can be obtained
at www.ICGtesting.com
Printed in the USA
BVHW021011220319
543444BV00019B/605/P